MW00892277

STOP SNORING GRANDPA!

By Kally Mayer

In a tiny little town
Under the street lamps glow,
Sits a pretty, yellow house
In the middle of the row.

Inside this yellow house,
Something is not quite right.
All the lights are on,
In the middle
of the night.

This is where I live,
With Baby Kate and Sister Sue.
Mom, Dad and Grandpa,
Fishy and Doggy too!

My Grandpa lives with us,
As he is very old.
We turn the heat up high,
So he doesn't get too cold.

There are some days,
When Grandpa gets a little gruff.
Cause he always forgets,
Where he puts all
his stuff!

Sometimes I play detective,
To see if I can find clues.
"Where did Grandpa
put his socks?
Oh, they're in his shoes!"

Grandpa likes to talk about,
When he was just a kid.
Growing up on the farm,
And all the chores he did!

I love to cuddle on Grandpa's lap,
As he reads me a book.
Or help him read the recipes,
When he decides to cook.

We all love our Grandpa,
But one thing we can't ignore.
At night, when the house is still,
Grandpa loves to snore!

The snoring starts out softly,
Then gradually gets so loud.
Sounds exactly like,
A giant thundercloud!

The snoring wakes us all up,
The house is filled with cries.
We're finding it hard to sleep,
Or even close our eyes!

Daddy doesn't wake up,
'Cause he is snoring too.
Not quite as loud as Grandpa.
Oh, what are we to do?

We are all wearing earmuffs,
Put blankets under the door.

Nothing seems to work,
As we hear Grandpa snore.

The windows start to shake,
And rattle and what's more,
The sound of Grandpa snoring,
Escapes right through the door.

The snores travel
down the street,
Land on the roof tops.
They wake up the
whole neighborhood,
We all wish it would stop!

Mommy never gets to sleep,
She stays awake all night.
Sips her tea and yawns,
Under the kitchen light.

The police chief comes to the door,
The fire chief and mayor too.
They complain about all the noise,
Not much that we can do!

During class it's hard,
Not to close my eyes.
Don't have energy at recess,
To play with all
the guys.

Mom sleeps during the day,
With Doggy and Baby Kate.
She often nods off,
Still chewing the breakfast she ate.

Our family doesn't
get much sleep.
Don't like to make a fuss,
But Grandpa's very loud snoring,
Is getting the best of us!

Then one day I came home,
To find my Grandpa gone.
Mom took him to the hospital,
Said he wouldn't be gone long.

That night I tossed and turned,
I tried to fall asleep.
The house was way too quiet,
You couldn't hear a peep.

Got up and went
to the kitchen.
To find my whole family.
Sitting at the table,
Awake and sipping tea.

Looked outside the window,
The neighbors had their lights on.
Wondered if they were missing,
My Grandpa's snoring sound.

I was worried about my Grandpa,
Hoped he'd be okay.
Guess we had gotten use to,
His snoring everyday!

Crept to my bedroom window,
Saw the moon shining bright.
Wondered what Grandpa was doing,
On this still and quiet night.

Grandpa was gone awhile,
As he was very sick.
I counted the days
on the calendar,
Each day got a tick.

W hen Grandpa
finally came home,
We all gave him
a hug and kiss.
Threw him a big party,
To show him how
much he was missed.

Now no one seems to notice,

Or complain much anymore.

Seems we all love to hear.

My Grandpa when he snores!

Now in this tiny little town,
Under the street lamp light.
Sits a pretty yellow house,
Where the family all sleeps tight!

The End

Stop Snoring Grandpa!

© Copyright 2014 by *Kally Mayer*

Reproduction or translation of any part of this work beyond that permitted by section 107 or 108 of the 1976 American Copyright Act without permission of the copyright owner is unlawful. Requests for permission or further information should be addressed to the author.

This publication is designed to provide accurate and authoritative information in regard to the subject matter covered. It is sold the understanding that the publisher is not engaged in rendering legal, accounting, or other professional services. If legal advice or other expert assistance is required, the services of a competent professional person should be sought.

First Published, 2014

Printed in United States

46865727R00021

Made in the USA
Middletown, DE
11 August 2017